Hands
are not for
Hurting

ISBN: 978-1-60169-222-1

Published by innovativeKids®
A division of innovative USA®, Inc.
50 Washington St.
Norwalk, CT 06854
iKids is a registered trademark in Canada and Australia.

www.innovativekids.com

Printed in USA
3 5 7 9 10 8 6 4

My hands can do so many things!

My hands can
draw a picture.

My hands can share a snack.

My hands can throw
a ball . . .

. . . and my hands
can pet a dog!

My friend Billy has hands that can hurt.

He hits when he wants a toy.

He pulls when he wants to get somewhere first.

He pinches when he gets mad.

I tell my mom that I don't want
Billy's hands to hurt me anymore.
She says that some kids hit when
they don't know what to do or say.

Mom says that my helping hands can show Billy's hurting hands how he can be a better friend.

At school, I show Billy all the neat things his hands can do.

I show him how to say hello and good-bye in sign language.

I show him how to shake hands
and high-five.

I show Billy how to use his
hands to make cool shapes, like
circles, triangles, and even hearts.

I show Billy that instead of hitting when he wants a toy, he can use his hands to play a game while he waits his turn.

I show Billy that instead of pulling to be first in line, he can tap a rhythm on his knees.

When ' ' I show him
- he can
...ands
...t to ten.

words to say
how ...ad of pinching.

Billy and I use our hands to play a board game.

He plays so nicely that Ms. Green lets him choose a song to sing at music time.

We clap our hands and snap our fingers while we sing along.

17

We use our hands to play
basketball with the whole class!

Now Billy's hands can do a lot
of neat things, just like mine.

Now everyone wants to play with Billy.

Especially me.

A Note to Parents

Use the CAAMP method to help your child learn appropriate ways to express himself or herself.

The CAAMP method is a way to promote pro-social behavior and help your child understand that it is not okay to hit. CAAMP stands for Communication, Acknowledgment, Alternatives, Modeling, and Praise. These five words are the basis for helping you teach your child not to hit when he or she is upset or not getting what he or she wants.

| Communication | Acknowledgment | Alternatives | Modeling | Praise |

Communication

Communicate with your child in a way that will help him or her hear and listen to you. When telling your child that it is not appropriate to hit others and to use his or her words instead,
- use your child's name
- make eye contact with and be at eye level with your child
- do not repeat things; be simple and direct
- have your child repeat what you stated or, if he or she is not able to, ask your child a simple question about what you stated
- praise your child for good listening, and remind him or her that it is not okay to hit

Acknowledgment

Acknowledging your child's feelings and helping to label those feelings is extremely important. Validate that it is okay to get angry sometimes, but it is not okay to hit others. Help your child to identify his or her primary emotions (i.e., angry, happy, sad, excited, scared, and frustrated), and encourage your child to talk to you when he or she is feeling a certain emotion. Remember, no emotion is bad. However, engaging negative behaviors in response to those emotions is inappropriate. Many more emotions can be identified as your child gets older.

Alternatives

Teach your child alternatives to hitting and ways to make himself or herself feel calm. You can suggest many alternatives to your child, such as talking to a parent or teacher about what he or she is mad about, holding a favorite toy/stuffed animal, using words to tell a person how he or she feels, drawing a picture of how he or she feels, or walking away and taking a time-out. You can also help your child calm down when he or she is angry. For very young children, this may involve distracting your child by engaging him or her in an activity or speaking to him or her about an upcoming event. For slightly older, preschool-age children, this may include getting your child to take deep breaths or closing his or her eyes and thinking about a favorite activity.

Modeling

As caretakers, our actions are one of the most important ways to encourage pro-social behaviors while discouraging hitting. Children model what they see. If a child sees others hit in his or her home, then he or she will learn to hit from example. Therefore, it is extremely important for you to model appropriate behavior. When you become angry, point out and label your emotions. Inform your child that you did not hit anyone but found another way to release your frustration instead.

Praise

Verbally praise your child for engaging in pro-social behaviors and for doing something other than hitting when he or she is frustrated. Children tend to respond to attention. Often, hitting and acting out gets them attention, although it is negative. Observe your child's behaviors: If he or she is doing something other than hitting, let your child know that you are proud he or she is using an alternative. If your child feels as though he or she is being recognized and receiving attention, you will be shaping your child's behavior away from hitting and toward more appropriate behaviors.

Sammi Gureasko-Moore, Ph.D.
Nationally Certified School Psychologist

Look at my Hands

Look at my hands as they wave hello to you.

Look at my hands as they play peek-a-boo.

My hands can be quiet, folded in my lap.

My hands can be loud; clap, clap, clap!

The fingers on my hands can wiggle to and fro.

And as I get bigger, my hands begin to grow.

Sometimes I get the feeling that my hands may push or hit.

But I say NO to hurting hands. I stop and think and sit.

No matter what I'm feeling—sad, or mad, or blue,

Hands are not for hurting; there's more that hands can do!

Look at my hands as they dribble a ball.

Look at my hands as they build a tower tall.

My hands can be gentle, with cuddles for my cat.

My hands can hit a homer with a whack of my bat.

Look at my hands as they wave good-bye to you.

Can you think of more that your hands do?